Baby Lamb Is Hungry

Annette Smith
Illustrated by Samantha Asri

Josh and Lily are at the farm.

"Josh! Lily!" said Grandpa.
"Come and see the baby lamb."

"I can not see a baby lamb," said Josh.

"I can see the mother sheep," said Lily.

"Look down here," said Grandpa. "The baby lamb is down here in the grass."

Baa-baa. Baa-baa.

"Is the baby lamb hungry?" said Josh.

Baa-aa! Baa-aa!

"The baby lamb is looking for milk," said Grandpa.

"Look at the baby lamb's tail," said Lily.

"The baby lamb is happy," said Josh.